This is young Debra,
and Debra has got
a family who are
a talented lot.

3

This is her dad –
he's a big, funny clown;
always mucking about,
always fooling around.

This is her mum –
she can walk the hire wire
while juggling skittles
and breathing out fire.

This is her brother –
an expert with spoons,
and making strange animals
out of balloons.

TAK
ATTAK
ATTAK
ATTAK

And even her hamster,
her dog and her cat
perform a magnificent
acrobat act.

But what about Debra?

What tricks could she do?

She couldn't do any

as far as she knew.

She couldn't do clowning …

or bending balloons …

or juggling
skittles …

or playing
with spoons.

While her mother made
walking the tightrope look easy,
the very idea made poor Debra
feel queasy.

"Don't worry, dear Debra,"
the others would say.
"We're sure you'll find out
what you're good at one day."

Poor Debra, dear Debra,

she feels such a fool.

And things aren't much better

when she goes to school.

Each morning, she finds

in her coat, up her sleeve;

a big bunch of flowers
that make Teacher sneeze!

15

When she opens her desk,

all the other kids shriek,

"It's another white rabbit,

the fifth one this week!"

When she opens her lunchbox
to see what is there,
a flock of white doves
flaps up into the air.

"This silly behaviour
will simply not do,"
says the teacher to Debra.
"This school's NOT a zoo!

Now pack up your things, girl,
I think that you should
go away for a while
till you've learned to be good!"

As Debra creeps off
with big tears in her eyes,
a little boy jumps on his chair
and he cries:

"Oh, please don't be sad,
don't be gloomy and tragic.
Whatever they say, Debra,
I think you're MAGIC!"

"Magic!" cries Debra.

"That's JUST what I am!"

Then she dashes back home

just as fast as she can.

She flies through the door
and knocks Dad for six,
"I'm AbracaDEBRA!
I do magic tricks!"

23

"At last!" cry the others.
"You know who you are!
Let's pack up the tent
and get into the car!"

They pack up the tent
and away they all go;
to travel the world
with their own special show.

And they put on a show,
the best show that they could,
and everyone thinks
they are terribly good.

But the one they like most

(as I'm sure you have guessed)

is ABRACADEBRA!

They like her the best!

28

29

Puzzle 1

Put these pictures in the correct order.
Now try writing the story in your own words!

Puzzle 2

Choose the correct speech bubbles for each character. Can you think of any others? Turn over to find the answers.

Answers

Puzzle 1

The correct order is: 1f, 2c, 3b, 4e, 5d, 6a

Puzzle 2

Debra: 3, 4

Teacher: 1, 6

Little boy: 2, 5

Look out for more great Hopscotch stories:

My Dad's a Balloon
ISBN 978 0 7496 9428 9*
ISBN 978 0 7496 9433 3

Bless You!
ISBN 978 0 7496 9429 6*
ISBN 978 0 7496 9434 0

Marigold's Bad Hair Day
ISBN 978 0 7496 9430 2*
ISBN 978 0 7496 9435 7

Mrs Bootle's Boots
ISBN 978 0 7496 9431 9*
ISBN 978 0 7496 9436 4

How to Teach a Dragon Manners
ISBN 978 0 7496 5873 1

The Best Den Ever
ISBN 978 0 7496 5876 2

The Princess and the Frog
ISBN 978 0 7496 5129 9

I Can't Stand It!
ISBN 978 0 7496 5765 9

The Truth about those Billy Goats
ISBN 978 0 7496 5766 6

Izzie's Idea
ISBN 978 0 7496 5334 7

Clever Cat
ISBN 978 0 7496 5131 2

"Sausages!"
ISBN 978 0 7496 4707 0

The Truth about Hansel and Gretel
ISBN 978 0 7496 4708 7

The Queen's Dragon
ISBN 978 0 7496 4618 9

Plip and Plop
ISBN 978 0 7496 4620 2

Find out more about all the Hopscotch books at:
www.franklinwatts.co.uk

*hardback